These pants belong to:

(Write your name here)

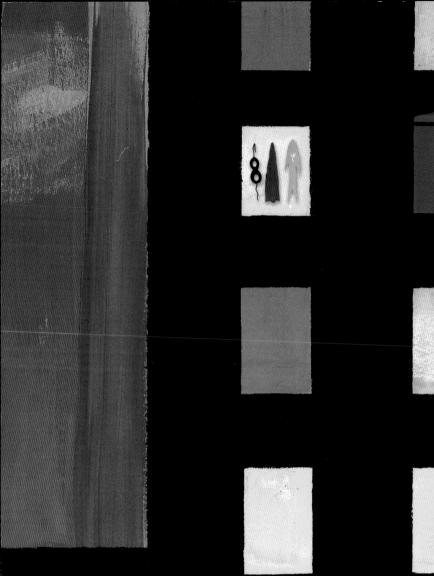
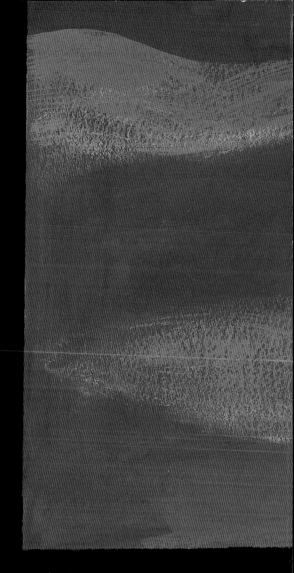

OXFORD
UNIVERSITY PRESS

Great Clarendon Street, Oxford OX2 6DP

Oxford University Press is a department of the University of Oxford. It furthers
the University's objective of excellence in research, scholarship, and education by
publishing worldwide. Oxford is a registered trade mark of Oxford University Press
in the UK and in certain other countries

Text © Timothy Knapman 2015
Illustrations © Rosie Reeve 2015
Title lettering © 2015 Sunplash. All Rights Reserved. P22 Type foundry,
Inc. http://www.p22.com

The moral rights of the author and illustrator have been asserted
Database right Oxford University Press (maker)

First published in 2015

British Library Cataloguing in Publication Data
Data available

ISBN: 978 0 19 273229 9 (hardback)
ISBN: 978 0 19 273723 6 (paperback)
ISBN: 978 0 19 273724 3 (eBook)

10 9 8 7 6 5 4 3 2 1

Printed in China

Paper used in the production of this book is a natural, recyclable product made
from wood grown in sustainable forests. The manufacturing process conforms to
the environmental regulations of the country of origin.

To Andrew, Daniel,
and Ben with love
TK

To Karen, Peter,
Jodie, and Julian
RR

MIGHTY SMALL

TIMOTHY KNAPMAN

ROSIE REEVE

OXFORD
UNIVERSITY PRESS

This is Max Small.

All his life,
from when he was a
mighty
tiny baby . . .

to a
mighty
titchy toddler . . .

to a
mighty
small mouse . . .

Max has had a
mighty
BIG
secret.

Bad Cat

Max is Mighty Small ...

Superhero!

He wasn't faster than a speeding bumblebee.

zz --- --- ZZ --- --- ZZ ---

He couldn't leap mighty obstacles in a single leap.

h-i-p-p-e-t-y h-o-p-p-e-t-y

Splat!

And he could only be invisible if he was standing behind something big enough.

'I must have a superpower,' thought Max. 'And there's only one way to find out what it is!'

But he had a cape. And he always wore his underpants over his trousers.

(When his mum wasn't looking.)

So the Hamster Gangsters used him for fruit-throwing target practice.

Splat!

Splurge!

And the squirrel stick-up men pinched his pants and left him tied to a daffodil.

Oh, Pants!

'I'm not **Mighty** Small,' said Max sadly. 'I'm just small.'

And he hung up his cape and stopped being a superhero.

UNTIL . . .

the circus came to town.
The band oompahed down
Main Street.

There were fire-eaters and fireworks for the great parade.
And the townspeople were so excited that . . .

no one noticed Sam the Strongman bending the bars of the bank so he could steal all the bags of gold . . .

and toss them to Tottering Tom the Tightrope Walker, who tiptoed high

Max was so scared, but he just couldn't let them get away!

So he put
on his suit
and cape . . .

his little
boots . . .

his gloves . . .

and his mask.
And that made
him feel braver.

Then he leapt into action, crying,

'BADDIE PANTS BEWARE!

Yee-Harr!

But the clowns
didn't hear him.

So Max jumped on the back of the unicycle.

VROOM!

And held on
tight . . .

all the way back to their Big Top hide-out.
Where the Boss, Mr Big, was waiting
to fill his trunk with gold.

'**I'm rich!**'
Cried Mr Big.
'**It's all MINE!**
If anyone says otherwise
I will squish them flat!'

Max suddenly
felt very cold and alone.
But then the circus lights
gave
him another
Mighty
superhero idea.

and they fell over in a
great big heap.

And he went stomping towards Max.

'Aaarrrgh!' shrieked Mr Big. 'It's a mouse!'

'What's wrong, Boss?' said Sam the Strongman.

'What's wrong, Boss?' said Tightrope Tom.

'Don't you know, elephants are terrified of mice?' giggled the Clowns.

Mr Big was so scared that he gave back all the gold. He begged the police to lock him up in a nice safe prison far away from Max.

And he took just enough gold
to buy a new pair of underpants.

Spangly ones!

The end . . . ?